The Fairy and the Woodcutter

선녀와 나무꾼

글 | 삐아제영어연구원 그림 | 심수근 감수 | Mark Trevena

Once upon a time,
a good woodcutter lived
with his mother.

One day, the woodcutter met a deer.
The deer was driven away by a hunter.
"Mr. Woodcutter. Please help me,"
The deer said.
He hid the deer.

The deer thanked him a lot.
"Mr. Woodcutter. In the pond,
hide a celestial robe of a fairy.
And get married with the owner.
But don't give it back before you have
three children."

The woodcutter went to the pond.
He hid a fairy's clothes.

The fairy whose clothes he took
couldn't go back up.

11

The woodcutter
got married with her.
He was really happy.

She's given birth to two children.
So, the woodcutter showed
the fairy her clothes.

But the fairy put on her
celestial robe,
held the children in
and went up to the sky.
The woodcutter bounced on
the ground and regretted
his decision.

At that time, the deer appeared.
"Why did you show her the clothes?
Soon, a well bucket will come from the sky.
Get in and go up to the sky."

The woodcutter got in the well bucket.

He met his wife and children in the sky.

He was happy.

The woodcutter missed his mother.

His wife gave him a swift horse.
"Mother, mother!"

His mother gave a porridge her son liked.
The woodcutter dropped hot porridge
by mistake on the horse's back.
The surprised horse went up to the sky alone.

The woodcutter missed his
wife and children.
Finally, he just looked up to
the sky and cried.
After he died, he became
a rooster.

선녀와 나무꾼

정말 선녀를 만날 수 있는 연못이 있다면 가 보고 싶지 않을까요?

그리고 아름다운 선녀를 아내로 맞이할 수 있다면 참 기쁘겠지요.

그러려면 이 이야기처럼 착한 나무꾼의 마음을 가져야 합니다.

우리 조상들의 선한 마음이 이 이야기의 근본입니다.

사슴은 목숨을 구해 준 은인에게 선녀와 결혼할 방법을 알려 줍니다.

사슴의 말대로 선녀와 결혼했지만 나무꾼은 실수로

다시는 선녀와 아이들을 만나지 못하게 됩니다.

그리고 죽은 후에 닭이 되어서까지 하늘을 향해 우는

나무꾼의 애절함이 우리를 더욱 슬프게 만듭니다.

사랑하는 사람과 헤어진다면 그것보다 슬픈 일은 없을 거예요.

그러니 여러분도 자신에게 주어진 행복을 지키기 위해서

꼭 명심해야 할 것이 있다는 것을 잊지 마세요.

재미 술술
이야기 꾸미기

그림 순서대로 이야기를 꾸며 보세요.
앞에서 읽은 이야기를 떠올려서 말하거나,
새로운 이야기를 만들어도 좋아요.

The Fairy and the Woodcutter
선녀와 나무꾼

Once upon a time, a good woodcutter lived with his mother.

One day, the woodcutter met a deer.
The deer was driven away by a hunter.
"Mr. Woodcutter. Please help me,"
The deer said.
He hid the deer.

The deer thanked him a lot.
"Mr. Woodcutter. In the pond,
hide a celestial robe of a fairy.
And get married with the owner.
But don't give it back before you have three children."

The woodcutter went to the pond.
He hid a fairy's clothes.

The fairy whose clothes he took couldn't go back up.

The woodcutter got married with her.
He was really happy.

She's given birth to two children.
So, the woodcutter showed
the fairy her clothes.

옛날 옛날에
착한 나무꾼이 어머니를 모시고 살았어요.

어느 날, 나무꾼은 사냥꾼에게 쫓기는 사슴을 만났어요.
"나무꾼님, 저 좀 살려 주세요."
나무꾼은 사슴을 숨겨 주었어요.

사슴은 나무꾼이 무척 고마웠어요.
"나무꾼님, 연못에서 선녀의 날개옷 하나를 감추고 아내로 맞으세요.
그런데 아이 셋을 낳기 전에 절대로 옷을 돌려 주시면 안돼요."

나무꾼은 연못을 찾아갔어요.
나무꾼은 선녀의 날개옷 하나를 감추었어요.

날개옷을 잃어버린 한 선녀는 하늘로 올라가지 못했어요.

나무꾼은 선녀를 아내로 맞았습니다.
나무꾼은 무척 행복했습니다.

선녀가 아이 둘을 낳았어요.
나무꾼은 아내에게 날개옷을 보여 주었어요.

But the fairy put on her celestial robe,
held the children in and went up to
the sky.
The woodcutter bounced on the ground and
regretted his decision.

At that time, the deer appeared.
"Why did you show her the clothes?
Soon, a well bucket will come from
the sky. Get in and go up to the sky."

The woodcutter got in the well bucket.
He met his wife and children in the sky.
He was happy.
The woodcutter missed his mother.

His wife gave him a swift horse.
"Mother, mother!"

His mother gave a porridge her son liked.
The woodcutter dropped hot porridge
by mistake on the horse's back.
The surprised horse went up to the sky alone.

The woodcutter missed his wife and children.
Finally, he just looked up to the sky
and cried.
After he died, he became a rooster.

그러나 날개옷을 입은 선녀는 아이를 안고서 하늘로 올라갔
어요.
나무꾼은 땅을 치며 후회의 눈물을 흘렸어요.

그때, 예전의 그 사슴이 나타났어요.
"왜 날개옷을 보여주셨어요?
 그 연못으로 하늘에서 두레박이 내려올 테니 그걸
타고 하늘로 올라가세요."

나무꾼은 두레박을 타고 하늘로 올라가 아내와
아이들을 만났어요.
행복한 시간을 보내던 나무꾼은 어머님이 보고
싶었어요.

아내가 용마 한 필을 구해 주었어요.
"어머니, 어머니"

어머니는 아들이 좋아하는 팥죽을 주었어요.
나무꾼이 실수로 뜨거운 팥죽을 말 등에 떨어뜨렸어요.
깜짝 놀란 말은 하늘로 올라가버렸습니다.

나무꾼은 아내와 자식들이 너무나 그리웠어요.
결국 나무꾼은 하늘만 쳐다보며 울다가 죽어서 닭이 되었답
니다.